# The Tree House

*...og was four, and William was seven, and their new ...e had only just been built. But the tree at the bottom ...he garden was a hundred years old. It was the ...est tree Sprog had ever seen.*

...og and William are so excited when Dadda says ...vill build them a tree house in the old chestnut t... . There is even a tea chest to use for a cabin. It i... oing to be the best tree house ever. But then ...da has to go to America to work—for six whole ...ths! However will they get the tree house ...hed without him? Dadda promises to send them ...esent for the tree house every month until he ...es home—but the best present of all would ...) have Dadda home for Christmas.

...n Cross has been writing for children for many ..., and her books have won the Carnegie Medal, the ...ties Book Prize, and Whitbread Children's Novel ...rd. Her best-selling books about The Demon ...lmaster have been made into a hugely popular BBC ...ision series. She is married with four children, and l... in Warwickshire. Her hobbies include orienteering ar... laying the piano.

# The Tree House

OTHER OXFORD FICTION

# THE TREE HOUSE

Gillian Cross

Illustrated by Lesley Harker

**OXFORD**
UNIVERSITY PRESS

# OXFORD

UNIVERSITY PRESS

Great Clarendon Street, Oxford OX2 6DP

Oxford University Press is a department of the University of Oxford.
It furthers the University's objective of excellence in research, scholarship,
and education by publishing worldwide in

Oxford    New York

Auckland   Cape Town   Dar es Salaam   Hong Kong   Karachi
Kuala Lumpur   Madrid   Melbourne   Mexico City   Nairobi
New Delhi   Shanghai   Taipei   Toronto

With offices in

Argentina   Austria   Brazil   Chile   Czech Republic   France   Greece
Guatemala   Hungary   Italy   Japan   Poland   Portugal   Singapore
South Korea   Switzerland   Thailand   Turkey   Ukraine   Vietnam

Oxford is a registered trade mark of Oxford University Press
in the UK and in certain other countries

British Library Cataloguing in Publication Data available

ISBN: 978-0-19-275293-2

Typeset by AFS Image Setters Ltd, Glasgow

Printed and bound by
CPI Group (UK) Ltd., Croydon, CR0 YY

Paper used in the production of this book is a natural,
recyclable product made from wood grown in sustainable forests.
The manufacturing process conforms to the environmental
regulations of the country of origin.

For Anthony and Katy

# Contents

## Chapter 1

### The Chestnut Tree

Sprog was four, and William was seven, and their new house had only just been built.

But the tree at the bottom of the garden was a hundred years old.

It was the biggest tree Sprog had ever seen. The day they moved into the house, he went down the garden and stood underneath the big, spreading branches, staring up. Up and up.

William followed Sprog down the garden, but he didn't waste any time staring. As soon as he saw the tree, he yelled.

'Dadda! Come and look! We can have a tree house!'

Their father bounded down the garden, just like William, only twice as fast. But when he saw the tree, he stopped, very still.

'It's a sweet chestnut tree,' he said softly. 'Next winter we can roast chestnuts together. The way *I* did with *my* dad.'

William wasn't interested in chestnuts. 'What about the *tree house*?'

Dadda grinned and studied the tree. 'It looks perfect. The platform could go *there*—where the branches divide. And maybe the removal men would sell me a tea chest. To make a little cabin at one end.'

'And can we have a ladder?' William said, bouncing up and down with excitement.

'Don't see why not.' Dadda pulled a bit of paper out of his pocket, and began to sketch the shape of the tree. 'The cabin could go there—'

William's eyes gleamed. 'Could you cut windows in it?'

'Of course. And Mam might make you some curtains—'

Sprog looked up at the bare, wintry tree and imagined it all. The branches would rustle round the tree house, and when the leaves grew they would hide it.

'Can we really have one?' he whispered. '*Really?*'

Dadda looked down and smiled. 'Not straight away. There's wallpapering to do first, and shelves to put up. But I won't forget. We'll make it in the summer.'

They planned it in the evenings. Sometimes Dadda had to go away to work, but whenever he was at home he got out the tree house drawings before Sprog and William went to bed. The four of them sat round, deciding how to paint the little cabin, and what to do with the rest of the platform.

William was impatient. 'All we ever do is talk about it. Why can't we *make* it?'

'Everything's got to be planned,' Mam said. 'Look at those shelves I put up yesterday. If I hadn't planned them properly, they'd have fallen down by now.'

'The tree house'll never fall down,' William said, darkly. 'Because it's never going to be built.'

Dadda growled at him. 'Don't *nag*. I'll build it when the fine weather comes.'

Sprog didn't nag. But when William was at school, and he was all on his own, he went into the garage to look at the tea chest that was going to be the cabin. He ran his fingers along the pale, smooth planks Dadda had bought for the floor.

And he wished.

Then one day, in the middle of July, Dadda came home early. He kissed Sprog, winked, and disappeared into the garage. When Sprog and Mam set off to fetch William from school, they heard loud sawing noises.

Sprog squeezed Mam's hand and looked up at her. He was too excited to say anything, but she understood. She smiled down at him and squeezed back.

When they got home again, there was a metal ladder propped against the chestnut tree. Dadda was up in the branches with the floor planks. Hammering.

William dropped his lunch box by the gate and ran straight down the garden. 'Fantastic! Can I come up and look?'

Dadda stuck his head out between the long, jagged leaves, and growled his terrible Ferocious Monster growl. 'If any boys come up this ladder, I'LL EAT THEM WITH MUSTARD!'

William danced round the tree. 'What about the cabin? And our wooden ladder? You haven't forgotten, have you?'

There were no answers. Only growls and hammering.

Sprog pulled at Mam's sleeve. 'Can we have our drinks in the garden?'

Mam chuckled. 'I'll bring them out. Don't let William get in Dadda's hair.'

She picked up the lunch box and disappeared into the house, and Sprog ran down the garden. William was at the bottom of the ladder now, with one foot on the first rung. Sprog wondered how he would stop him if he really started to climb.

But it was all right. The Ferocious Monster stuck its head out of the tree again and grinned. 'What are you waiting for? Come on up. *Carefully*.'

William was up the ladder in a flash. Sprog went more slowly, holding on hard with both hands.

'It's brilliant!' William shouted. 'Look, Sprog!'

Sprog hauled himself up and looked round—and his mouth fell open.

He was on a wide platform in the very centre of the tree, hidden by long, jagged leaves. All round were long, yellow catkins, like furry caterpillars.

'It's *wonderful*!' he whispered.

And then the phone rang.

It was down at the bottom of the tree, lying on the lid of the toolbox. Dadda swung himself on to the ladder.

'Stay here, you two,' he said. 'Don't move an inch—OR I'LL FRY YOU

FOR BREAKFAST!' He rattled down the ladder, picked up the phone and grinned. 'Hi! Dennis?'

By the time he rang off, Mam was coming, with four mugs on a tray. Dadda bounded up the garden towards her, grinning wildly.

'Emma! I've got that American contract!'

Mam took a deep breath and put the tray down. 'That's wonderful. How long is it for? And when do you have to leave?'

'I leave the day after tomorrow.' Dadda grabbed a mug from the tray. 'For six months.'

Sprog blinked. He didn't understand.

But William did. He went bright red. 'You can't go! You haven't made our tree house!'

Dadda stopped smiling. 'I've got to, Will. It's work.'

'It's stupid work!' shouted William. 'Change your job!'

'You don't need to fuss,' Mam said. 'I can finish the tree house for you.'

William looked sulky. '*Dadda's* doing it. He promised.'

Dadda sighed. 'Look—I *have* to go. But suppose I fix the tea chest up here tonight? Then you'll have a cabin.'

'What about the windows?' said William. 'And the door?'

'I'll make those when I come back.'

Sprog twisted one of the long, yellow catkins round his finger. 'Summer will be over by then.'

'You can play in the tree house without windows and doors,' Dadda said gently. 'I'll send you other things instead. How about that? A tree house parcel every month?'

'Promise?' said William.

'Promise!' said Dadda.

Sprog let go of the catkin and watched it drop to the ground. 'Will you be back in time to roast the chestnuts?' he said.

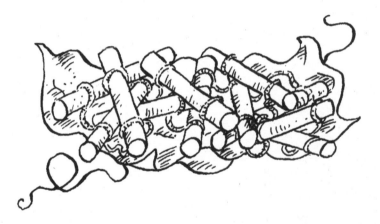

## Chapter 2

## The First Parcel

It was three weeks before the first parcel came. By that time, William had got very good at climbing up into the tree house.

'Why don't you do it too, Sprog?' he kept saying. 'It's easy. Put your left foot on this bump here and hold on to these broken branches. Then lift your right foot to here—'

But Sprog couldn't. He could put his left foot on the first bump all right, and hold the two branches. But as soon as he looked up, the tree house seemed horribly high. And he just *couldn't* lift his other foot off the ground.

There was no other way of getting into the tree house. Mam said the metal ladder was too dangerous for them to use on their own. So Sprog had to stand at the bottom of the tree, while William shouted down at him.

'It's wonderful! This tree is big enough to make a *castle*! Why don't you come up, Sprog?'

Sprog wanted to, more than anything else in the world. But whenever he looked up at the tree house, he knew it was impossible. If he tried, his feet would slip, or the branches he was holding would crack, and he would fall. He *couldn't*.

Then the parcel came.

The postman rang at eleven o'clock one Saturday morning, and William and Sprog opened the door together. The moment they saw their names on the parcel, they knew who it was from.

'Dadda!' shouted William.

He began to rip off the paper. Sprog picked up the string and wound it neatly round his fingers, but when Mam came downstairs there was brown paper all over the floor.

And William was holding a jumble of ropes and wooden rods. He frowned at it.

'What is it, Mam?'

Mam grinned. 'You'll see.' She took hold of two ends and went backwards up the stairs, pulling the ropes out straight. Sprog's eyes opened wide as the thing untangled.

'It's a rope ladder! *So I can get into the tree house!*'

William's eyes gleamed. 'Fix it up, Mam! *Please!*'

Mam looked at them. 'Maybe. When I've picked the rest of the raspberries.'

'But there's millions of raspberries!' William groaned. 'It'll take *hours*. Please do the rope ladder first!'

'No.' Mam shook her head. 'I want to

make some jam to take to Gran's tomorrow. Raspberries first.'

William's face went bright red.

'We can help with the raspberries,' Sprog said quickly. 'Then you'll get finished sooner.'

'All right.' Mam took three plastic bowls out of the cupboard. 'As long as you really help, and don't just eat the raspberries.'

'We promise!' William said. 'Come on, Sproggo!'

He seized one bowl and ran down the garden. By the time Sprog got there, he had already picked ten raspberries.

But it was a very hot day. By the time his bowl was half full, William was tired of raspberry-picking. He emptied the raspberries into Mam's bowl and ran off towards the chestnut tree.

Sprog went on working. Slowly and doggedly, he picked his way up each row and down the other side, without eating a single raspberry. He got very thirsty, and rather tired, but he filled his bowl four times.

'You've done well,' Mam said, as she weighed the raspberries.

*What about the rope ladder, then?* thought Sprog. But he didn't say it. He just stared up at her.

Mam laughed. 'Don't worry. I'm coming. I'll just go and get the tools.'

Running down the garden, Sprog called up into the tree. 'William! Mam's coming now! She's going to do it!'

But the tree house was empty.

'William?'

'I'm *here*,' said William's voice. 'Higher up.'

Sprog tilted his head back. William was perched on a high branch, way above the tree house. 'What are you doing up there?'

'Keeping watch,' William said. 'I can see for *miles*.'

'But how did you get *up* there?'

'Climbed. But it was very difficult. Some of the branches kept breaking.

Look, Sprog—' William began to climb down again, very cautiously, '—it's really *easy* to get up to the tree house. And if you can do it without the rope ladder, we can—'

Sprog had a horrible feeling he knew what William was going to say. But before he said it, Mam came down the garden, with the rope ladder in one hand, and the tools in the other.

'Right, then,' she said. 'Let's get this fixed.'

William bounded towards her. 'We've changed our minds, Mam. We don't want it going up to the tree house, because we can climb that bit. Put it higher up.'

'*You* can climb that bit,' Mam said. 'But what about Sprog?'

'He can do it too!' William said excitedly. 'If he tries! Can't you, Sprog?'

'I—' Sprog swallowed. He looked up at the tree house. Then at William's face. 'I *might* be able to.'

Mam put down the tool bag. 'Let's see you do it.'

Sprog went up to the tree. Very carefully, just as he had before, he put his left foot on the bump at the bottom and held on to the two short branches. Then he looked up at the tree house. He was very tired, from picking the raspberries, and it looked further away than ever.

'Go *on*!' hissed William. 'If Mam puts the rope ladder higher up, we can make a watchtower at the top. Like in a castle.'

Sprog looked further up, at the place where William had been sitting. That was *very* high. When he looked back at the tree house, it didn't seem quite so bad.

'We could have a tree *castle*!' whispered William.

Slowly and carefully, Sprog pulled himself up, lifting his right foot off the ground until it found the second bump in the trunk. Then

he reached higher, for the next
stubby branch.

A moment later, he was sitting in the
tree house, grinning down at Mam. And
William was bouncing round the tree,
shouting.

'You did it, Sprog! You did it! We
can have a tree castle!'

That night, William wrote to Dadda:

Dear Dadda,
     The rope ladder is BRILLIANT!
We've made a watchtower! Thanks
a lot.
          Love from William and Sprog

He ran into Sprog's bedroom and
thrust it under his nose. Sprog just
managed to draw three wobbly, tired
kisses.

Then he fell asleep, and dreamed of
raspberries and castles.

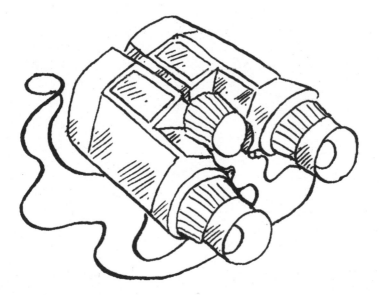

## Chapter 3

### *Enemies!*

In September, Sprog started school. On the first day, his teacher, Mrs Morrison, read a story about a magic, golden bird, and Sprog drew a picture of it, and sent it to Dadda.

Dear William and Sprog, (said Dadda's next letter)

Glad you liked the rope ladder. I liked Sprog's bird picture, too. It's up on my bedroom wall.

I thought the tree house might be a good place for bird-watching, so I'm sending you these.

Love, Dadda

Inside the parcel was a pair of binoculars.

William looked at them doubtfully. 'Bird-watching? In a *castle*?'

'Doesn't have to be birds,' said Mam. 'Take them up to your watchtower, and find out what you *can* see.'

William grinned at Sprog. 'Come on, Sir Stephen. Shall we go up to the castle and keep watch?'

'OK,' said Sprog.

William snorted. 'You don't say, *OK*. You say, *Verily, Sir William.*'

'Very lee, Sir William,' said Sprog obediently. He didn't know what it meant, but it sounded castleish, and he went on saying it every time William spoke to him.

'Let us climb up to the castle, Sir Stephen!'

'Very lee, Sir William.'

'Will you take the first watch in the tower?'

'Very lee, Sir William.'

'Don't forget the binoculars.'

26

'Very lee, Sir William.'

Hanging the binoculars round his neck, Sprog climbed the rope ladder. When he was settled in the watchtower, he looked through them.

'What do you see, Sir Stephen?' called William.

'Very lee, Sir William,' said Sprog.

William sighed. 'Don't *keep* saying that! Look through the binoculars and tell me what you can see.'

'Oh. OK.' Sprog looked. 'I can see lots of long brown things down on the grass.'

'Serpents?' said William hopefully.

Sprog frowned. 'No, I think they're the dead catkins off this tree.'

William sighed again. 'Look further away.'

'OK.' Sprog lifted the binoculars and scanned the garden. 'I can see Mam in the vegetable patch. She's digging up potatoes. And—oh, there's something *huge* behind her. Something big and orange and—'

'What?' William said, excitedly. 'Is it an alien?'

'I don't *think* so.' Sprog moved the binoculars a bit. 'Oh no. It's that pumpkin you're growing in your garden.'

'The *pumpkin*?' William screeched. 'Honestly, Sprog, you're *useless* at playing castles.'

'But you told me to say what I could see—'

'I didn't mean what you *could* see. I meant—Oh, come down and let me have a go!'

Sprog climbed down and handed over the binoculars. William was up the rope ladder in a flash, calling down all sorts of excited messages.

'I can see an army coming from the north! And—' He swung round, '—a terrible dragon flying from the east. And three black knights on fire-breathing horses—'

Sprog looked out of the tree. He couldn't see any of those things.

28

Perhaps he hadn't been using the binoculars right.

'And another army in the west!' yelled William. 'We need help! Go and find reinforcements! And ammunition!'

Slowly, Sprog climbed down the tree. He wandered across to the vegetable patch and stood beside Mam as she stuck the fork into the earth.

'Mam, what are re—re—?'

'Reinforcements?' Mam picked up

the potatoes and dropped them into the wheelbarrow. 'We haven't got any of those. But there's some ammunition.' She waved her hand at a little pile of potatoes on the ground. 'Those are too green to eat. Find a bag, and you can take them to throw at your enemies.'

Sprog frowned. 'We haven't got any enemies.'

'Have a look in the kitchen,' said Mam. 'The best enemies make a loud noise when you throw potatoes at them.'

Sprog was puzzled, but he wandered into the kitchen, to look for a plastic bag. Mam kept them stuffed between the saucepan stand and the vegetable rack and, as he pulled one out, he knocked an apple off the rack.

It hit the top saucepan, with a CLANG.

*The best enemies make a loud noise when you throw potatoes at them . . .*

Sprog grinned. He stuffed the plastic bag into his pocket and picked up three big old saucepans from the rack. Then he went back into the garden.

William was still in the watchtower. He was facing away from Sprog and yelling at the top of his voice. 'Wild horsemen coming from the north-west! A mad bull charging from the east!'

Behind his back, Sprog moved quietly round the garden, hiding the saucepans behind bushes upside down. Then he filled his plastic bag with green potatoes and went to the bottom of the chestnut tree.

'Very lee, Sir William!' he called. 'I've got the ammunition, but I can't carry it up the tree.'

'Coming!' William scrambled all the way down, and took the carrier bag up to the platform. 'Brilliant! Go up to the watchtower and tell me where the enemies are. I'll do the firing.'

'Very lee.'

Sprog climbed the rope ladder and took the binoculars from the branch where William had hung them.

Carefully he scanned the garden, until he caught a glimpse of one of the hidden saucepans.

He pointed at the bush. 'There's an enemy in armour, hiding behind that!'

'Right!' William glanced up, to see which way Sprog was pointing, and then flung the first potato, straight at the bush. It hit the saucepan, with an enormous CLANG!! and bounced off.

William gasped. 'Sprog! There *is* someone there! Someone in armour!'

'And there's another one over there!' called Sprog.

The second potato bounced straight back towards them.

'They're firing at us too!' shouted William. 'Leave the watchtower, Sprog—I mean, Sir Stephen—and help me with these cannon balls.'

'Very LEE!' said Sprog.

He scrambled down the rope ladder and threw a potato straight at the largest saucepan. CLANG! He grinned.

He was beginning to understand about playing castles.

Dear Dadda, (William wrote that night)

It was a good thing you sent the binoculars. We had enemies all round today. There was a wonderful battle!

Love from

William and Sprog

He took the letter into Sprog's bedroom. 'Here you are. Put some kisses on the bottom.'

'I can do my *name* now,' Sprog said, sleepily. 'Mrs Morrison is showing me.' And he wrote

Sprog

very big, at the bottom.

## Chapter 4

### Long Distance

In October, there were two parcels, one for Sprog and one for William.

If you've got all those enemies round you (said Dadda's letter), I think you need a stock of food in the tree house.

Inside each parcel was a tall, round tin, full of toffees wrapped in gold paper.

'Supplies!' said William. 'We mustn't waste them, Sprog. There's a hole in the chestnut tree. We'll keep them there and eat one every day. Then they'll last for *ages*.'

'Very lee, Sir William,' said Sprog, rather sadly. He liked toffees.

But he didn't cheat. He put his tin with William's, in the hole behind the tree house cabin, and every day he took out just one gold-wrapped toffee and ate it, very slowly.

It was William who cheated. He kept thinking of reasons for eating extra toffees. After a week, his tin was empty, and he was looking longingly at Sprog's.

'Can't you give me *one*?' he said, as they sat in the cabin. 'Knights always shared their food with each other.'

Sprog frowned. He wanted to eat his toffees, but his tin was still three-quarters full, and it seemed mean to say no.

'OK. Just *one*.' He dropped a toffee into William's empty tin and William grinned and rattled the tin.

'Thanks, Sir Stephen. Makes a lot of noise, doesn't it?'

Sprog sucked his own toffee. 'I saw a

programme on television once. About how to make telephones out of tins.'

'I remember!' William's eyes lit up. 'Let's do it!'

Sprog shook his head. 'I've forgotten how.'

'But *I* haven't.' William shook the tin again. 'You make holes in the tins and join them together with string.'

'I've got some string.' Sprog pulled a bundle out of his anorak pocket. 'I saved it from the rope ladder parcel.'

William took the neatly rolled string and unwound a bit. 'This is perfect. It would make a really long telephone, right up to the watchtower. But—'

He looked at Sprog's tin.

Sprog looked, too. He wanted to make a telephone, but they couldn't do it until both the tins were empty.

'I'll count my toffees,' he said. He began to take them out, laying them in rows of four on the wooden floor. The gold paper gleamed in the shadows. 'One, two, three . . . '

When he put the last toffee down, he had made eight rows.

Thirty-two toffees.

'That's *millions*!' wailed William. 'If you only eat one a day, we'll never get our telephone!'

Sprog looked at the toffees glinting on the wood. 'They haven't *got* to be in a tin.'

William brightened. 'You could get a bag from Mam. And she could make the holes for us, as well.' He pushed the tins into Sprog's pockets. 'Why don't you go and ask her?'

Slowly and carefully, Sprog climbed down the tree and went into the kitchen. When Mam heard what he wanted, she smiled.

'I had a telephone like that when I was a little girl. You find a bag for your toffees, and I'll make the holes.'

Sprog put the tins on the kitchen table, and went across to the plastic bags. 'Mam—'

'Mmm?' Mam didn't look up. She was sorting through the toolbox.

Sprog pulled out a bag and looked at it. 'William's finished his toffees. Do you think I ought to share mine with him?'

'Only if you want to,' said Mam. She turned the first tin upside down and hammered a skewer hole in the bottom. 'They're *your* toffees.'

Sprog thought about it.

Mam made the second hole and held out the tins. 'There you are. Mind you don't scratch yourselves.'

'Thanks.' Sprog put the tins in his pockets. As he took them he made a decision. He grabbed a second plastic bag and ran back to the tree.

As soon as he reached the tree house, William held out his hands. 'Come on. Let's have the tins.'

Sprog handed them over. Then he turned round to pick up the toffees. He was going to share them out into two bags, while William was making the telephone.

But there weren't any toffees there.
Sprog blinked. 'William—'

'Hang on a minute,' said William. He was trying to get the string through the bottom of the second tin.

Sprog gulped. 'But my toffees—'

William pushed one of the tins at him. 'Who cares about *toffees*? Take this up to the watchtower, so we can test the telephone.'

Sprog wanted to argue, but he was used to doing what William said. Pushing the tin into his pocket, he began to climb, with the string   trailing behind him.

It was scratchy up in the watchtower. The chestnuts were growing now, and the prickly cases caught his face. Sprog pushed them out of the way and put the tin to his ear.

For a second, he couldn't hear anything. Then William pulled the string tight and spoke into the tin at the other end. Sprog heard a jumbled, buzzing noise.

Then words. Loud and clear. *Get the binoculars. Look at the pumpkin and tell me what you see.*

The *pumpkin*? Sprog hooked the telephone string over a branch and reached for the binoculars, which were hanging on the branch beside him. Then he scanned the garden, looking for the huge orange shape of the pumpkin.

There it was. And underneath—!

Nestling underneath the pumpkin, on its black polythene mat, were dozens of tiny gold lumps.

Sprog grabbed the telephone again. 'My toffees! They're under the pumpkin. They're—'

Then he remembered that wasn't the way knights talked. Taking a deep breath, he started again.

'Very lee, Sir William, there is golden treasure under the pumpkin.'

Putting the telephone to his ear, he heard a chuckle.

'Go and gather it up, Sir Stephen!' said William's voice.

Hanging up the binoculars on one branch, and the telephone on the next one, Sprog scrambled down to the tree house and grabbed his plastic bags.

Then he hesitated. 'Do you . . . want some toffees?'

William gave him a long, lordly stare. 'I have taken a vow to eat no more toffees. Until my father returns.'

'You have?'

Sprog didn't understand. But he knew he could keep his toffees and he hurried down to pick them up.

They fetched the pumpkin, too, that evening, because Mam said it had to be cut before the frosts came. William wouldn't let her cook it.

'I'm saving it until Dadda comes back. I'm going to write and tell him.'

He and Sprog did the letter together, sitting at the kitchen table.

Dear Dadda, (wrote William)
Thank you for the toffees. They were good, and so were the tins.

We've cut my pumpkin because the weather's getting bad. But we'll keep it till you come.
COME BACK SOON.
Love,
William

And at the bottom, Sprog wrote

love from Sprog

## Chapter 5

## *A Useless Present!*

The parcel that came in November was long and thin, and Dadda had drawn big, fat raindrops all over the letter inside.

Dear William and Sprog,
    You're having real autumn weather, are you? Maybe you'd like this, to help you get safely to the tree house. Hope you like it.
                                Love,    Dadda

PS. I'll be home as soon as I can manage it.

Sprog undid the string. When he opened the paper, he grinned. 'It's an umbrella. A big yellow one.'

'An *umbrella*?' William went bright red. 'Knights don't have umbrellas!'

He scowled and knocked it on to the floor.

Mam picked it up again. 'Maybe Dadda doesn't *know* the tree house is a castle. Have you told him?'

'I can't tell him everything!' William said crossly. 'It takes too much writing. He ought to be here. Then he'd know what was going on.'

'We can tell him about the castle today,' Sprog said. 'When we write and say thank you for the umbrella.'

William stamped his foot. 'I'm not *going* to say thank you for it. It's a useless present. He said he'd send us things for the tree house, and this hasn't got anything to do with that.'

'Maybe you ought to go upstairs,' Mam said, very quietly. 'Until you feel more sensible.'

William opened his mouth. Sprog thought he was going to argue, but he didn't. He changed his mind and marched upstairs to his bedroom, slamming the door behind him.

Sprog started to follow, but Mam shook her head.

'William needs to be on his own. Go and play in the garden.'

So Sprog trailed outside. He thought he'd go and look at the tree house. The weather had been so wild and windy that they hadn't been out in the garden for nearly a week.

He walked down to the chestnut tree, and grabbed hold of the two broken branches, ready to start climbing. But then he saw something brown and shiny in the grass at his feet. He bent down to pick it up and—OUCH! He pricked his fingers.

Sucking them, he crouched down, to see what had hurt him. It was the prickly outside of one of the chestnuts off the tree. It had fallen to the ground and burst open, to show the ripe, glossy nut inside.

Carefully, Sprog pulled the chestnut out and looked at it. It was a bit like a conker, but flat on one side and not so shiny. And the bottom point was covered with silky silver hair.

Sprog stroked it. Then he looked around, to see if there were any more.

Yes, there was one over there, right out of its prickles. And another one next to it. And another—

They were everywhere. The wind and rain must have brought them all down, because the ground under the tree was covered with brown chestnuts and prickly cases.

Sprog started to collect the chestnuts. Slowly and patiently he tracked backwards and forwards, picking them up and piling them into a big heap. Then, when he'd found them all, he stood back and looked at the heap.

What was he going to do with all those nuts?

If Dadda had been there, they could have roasted them. The way he did with *his* father.

But Dadda wasn't there.

Sprog frowned. He wanted to take the nuts up to the tree house and hide them there, but he didn't know how to carry them. His pockets weren't big enough, and if he put them in a bag he wouldn't be able to climb with it.

What he needed was a bag that could go up by itself.

Or *something* that could go up by itself . . .

He was beginning to have an idea. Slowly he walked back to the kitchen and put his head round the door.

'Mam. Can I take the umbrella down to the tree house?'

'If you like,' said Mam. But she looked surprised. 'Is it raining?'

'No, but—I need it for something. And I need some string, too.'

Mam gave him the string off the parcel. He could see she was curious, but she didn't say anything. Only, 'Be careful.'

As Sprog carried the umbrella down the garden, he worked out his plan. He had to do everything in the right order. The first thing was to fix the string.

He left the umbrella beside the heap of chestnuts and climbed up to the tree house, with the string in his pocket. He tied one end of the string to a branch above his head, and let the rest of it fall towards the ground.

Then he climbed down and opened the umbrella. Upside down. Scooping up the chestnuts, he dropped them in and then tied the other end of the string to the umbrella handle.

Right! Now it was time to test his invention.

Scrambling up to the tree house, he untied the top end of the string, leaving it looped over the branch above his head. Then he began to pull, slowly and steadily.

54

And up came the umbrella, bringing the chestnuts with it.

There was only just enough room for it to get through. Once it snagged on a dead branch, and Sprog had to lean down and snap the branch off. Once it looked as though it might tip up and send all the chestnuts tumbling back to the ground. But Sprog kept pulling, very carefully, and at last it reached the tree house, with all the chestnuts still on board.

Grinning, Sprog pulled it on to the platform. Then he reached into the hole behind the cabin, to find the plastic bag with his toffees in. There were two toffees left. He ate one and put the other in his pocket, for tomorrow. Then he began to unload the chestnuts into the empty bag.

He was just stuffing the bag back into the hole when William came racing down the garden, looking cheerful again.

'Hi, Sprog,' he said. Then his eyes opened wide. 'What are you *doing*?'

'Getting things up to the tree house,' said Sprog. 'It's my invention. Look.' He pushed the umbrella off the platform and lowered it carefully. 'Put something in.'

William's eyes gleamed. 'That's *fantastic*! You've made a hoist. We'll use it for—' He looked round, eagerly. 'Let's have some of these prickly things. They can be ammunition, to throw at our enemies.'

He filled the umbrella with the prickly cases from the chestnuts, but he wouldn't let Sprog pull them up. He insisted on climbing the tree to do it himself.

'Just wait till I tell Dadda!' he said, as he hauled on the string. 'This is the best present *ever*!'

They spent so long throwing chestnut prickles and hoisting more up that it was almost dark before they came in. But they still had time to write their letter.

William did the first bit.

Dear Dadda,

It's a brilliant present! Thank you. Knights don't mind rain (because of their armour) but they need to get things into the castle if enemies are all round.

YOU'LL SEE HOW WHEN YOU COME BACK.

Love,
William

Sprog drew a picture of how the umbrella worked, and wrote his own message.

We Played till it was dark

## Chapter 6

### Out in the Dark

Dear Sprog and William, (said Dadda's December letter)

If you play till it's dark, you might need these to get back to the house again.

Lots of love,<br>Dadda

PS. I *think* I'll be home for Christmas. Keep your fingers crossed!

Sprog pulled the paper off his parcel and gasped. 'A torch!'

'So's mine,' said William. 'And they've got four colours! Brilliant!'

He spun the front of his torch and it shone red, then yellow, then white, then green. 'Can I take it to school, Mam?'

Mam shook her head. 'It'll get broken. Leave it here, and you can play with it when you come home.'

Sprog stared at his torch. 'Will it be dark then?'

Mam smiled. 'Almost.'

It was. But it was raining, too. Sprog and Mam took the big black umbrella when they went to fetch William, but their coats were soggy before they got home.

'No playing outside this evening,' Mam said. 'You'll have to have the torches in your bedroom.'

William looked sulky. 'It won't be so good.'

'It'll have to do. I'll make some hot milk, and then you can go upstairs.'

They shut their bedroom door and turned off the light, but the darkness wasn't exciting. It was too cosy. They could hear Mam, making pastry in the kitchen, and when William shone his torch around they saw cars and teddies.

'Knights wouldn't shine their torches at teddies!' William said crossly.

'Did knights *have* torches?' said Sprog.

'Of course not!' William snapped. 'But they had candles. And lanterns. And bonfires, for sending signals.'

Sprog spun the head of his torch, watching the colours change. White . . . red . . . yellow . . . green . . . 'We could do signals.'

'What?' William wasn't listening. He was staring through the curtains at the chestnut tree. All the leaves had fallen off now, and the branches were bare and dark.

'We could do signals,' Sprog said. 'You know—red for one thing, and green for another and—'

'Yes!' William spun round, his eyes dancing in the torchlight. 'Let's do it now! The white light can be—oh, wait a minute.' He turned on the main light and snatched up a piece of paper and a pencil. 'I'll do a list for us to learn.'

'I *might* not be able to read all the words,' Sprog said cautiously.

'I'll tell you. Oh, come *on*.' William lay on the floor, and wrote feverishly, saying the words out loud.

*WHITE light means WHO'S THERE?*
*RED light means FRIEND.*
*YELLOW light means HELP!*
*GREEN light means ALL IS WELL.*

Sprog repeated it all, struggling to remember. 'Suppose they get muddled? What if I do red first, then change to green?'

William thought. 'That ought to mean something different. I know—' He bent over the paper and wrote again.

*RED then GREEN means COME AT ONCE. SOMETHING GOOD.*

Sprog grinned. 'So we can do lots more? If we mix all the colours up?'

'Millions!' said William happily. 'But let's practise these first. Go over there.'

Sprog stood with his back to the window, listening to the rain drumming on the glass. William turned off the light and climbed up to the top bunk.

'Me first,' he said. He shone a white light at Sprog.

*WHITE light means WHO'S THERE?* thought Sprog. But how did he answer? Green? Yellow? He tried yellow.

There was a snort from the top bunk. 'Don't be silly. That means *HELP*! You should have done red, for *FRIEND*.'

Red. Of course. Sprog screwed his eyes up, making himself remember. 'Let's try again.'

They went on practising, until Mam knocked on the door.

'Are you two in there? It's Sprog's bedtime.'

William pulled a face. 'But we're doing something.'

'*Bedtime*,' said Mam. 'Look how dark it is outside.'

Sprog peeped through the curtains. It was very dark. Even the chestnut tree was hard to see now. But—

'Oh! It's stopped raining!' he said.

William groaned longingly. 'Mam! Couldn't we—?'

'No,' said Mam. 'It's too late for Sprog to be out.'

Sprog peered into the darkness. He wasn't at all sure he *wanted* to be out there, even with his torch. But he could imagine how a torch would look, flitting down the garden and up into the tree house. If only—

'Can *William* go out?' he said suddenly. 'On his own? It's not too late for him.'

William yelped with glee, but Mam looked at Sprog.

'Wouldn't you mind?'

'Not if I can look through the window. You see—there's something special we could do.'

William understood at once. He grabbed his torch and looked pleadingly at Mam. '*Let* me!'

'We-ell . . . ' she hesitated. 'All right. Just for a second, while I finish off in the kitchen.'

William grinned and rattled down the stairs and Mam went too. Sprog pressed his nose to the window, waiting for a signal.

William's torch flickered down the garden and up the tree. Then it shone straight towards the window. White.

*WHITE light means WHO'S THERE?* This time, Sprog knew the answer. He shone red, for *FRIEND*.

William's light changed to green. *ALL IS WELL.* Sprog spun the front of his torch so that was green too, and shone it back. Then he waited for the next signal.

He was still waiting, when Mam came into the room with a plate of warm mince pies.

'Do you want one of these before you clean your teeth? They're really for Christmas, but we ought to test them.'

'Yum!' said Sprog. He took a pie, and looked out of the window. 'What about William?'

'I'm going to call him in now,' said Mam.

'Oh,' said Sprog. He was disappointed. They'd only just started signalling properly and now they'd have to stop. And it wouldn't be dark again for a whole *day*. Sadly, he bit into his mince pie as Mam went towards the door.

And then he had a wonderful idea.

'Mam! You don't have to go! I can do it!'

He picked up his torch, switched it to red and shone it through the window. Then he changed the colour and shone it again. Red, then green.

*COME AT ONCE. SOMETHING GOOD.*

It worked perfectly. William came running up the stairs before Sprog had finished his first mince pie.

Dear Dadda, (William wrote while Sprog was in the bath)

The torches are fantastic! WHITE means WHO'S THERE? RED means FRIEND. YELLOW means HELP! GREEN means

ALL IS WELL and RED then GREEN means COME AT ONCE. SOMETHING GOOD.

Love,
William

When Sprog got out of the bath, he fetched his felt pens and coloured a red square and a green square on the bottom of the letter. Then he wrote

red        green

this is the sign abot christmas do it please love sprog

red        green

## Chapter 7

## Christmas

On Christmas Eve, Sprog woke up and stared at the ceiling. For a moment, he didn't know why he felt so sad. Then he remembered.

Dadda wasn't there.

Tonight they'd be hanging up their stockings. Tomorrow they would go to church and then have Christmas dinner and presents at Grandma's house. But Dadda wouldn't be there.

It was awful, but Sprog didn't moan. He was too miserable.

It was William who moaned, from the moment he got up. He banged down to breakfast with odd socks on and his jumper back to front. While they were wrapping presents, he sulked and got the Sellotape tangled up. And he wouldn't make any place cards for Christmas dinner.

'Why should I? Who cares where we sit?'

'But we *always* have place cards,' said Sprog.

'We always have Dadda!' William said crossly. 'But we're not going to have *him*, are we?'

By lunchtime, even Mam was looking gloomy. But she didn't snap. She served up the fish and chips and then sat down, with her elbows on the table.

'This is no good, is it?' she said. 'We can't be unhappy at Christmas. Let's do something special this afternoon, to cheer ourselves up.'

'Like what?' said William.

'Like . . . like having a bonfire,' said Mam. 'We can bake potatoes in the ashes, and have scones and mince pies.

And we could make a pumpkin lantern, out of your pumpkin.'

'But he's saving that,' said Sprog. 'For when Dadda comes home.'

'No I'm not,' said William, loudly. His face was very red. 'I'm tired of waiting. Let's make a lantern.'

So they did. They scooped out the middle of the pumpkin, and Mam made a pumpkin pie, while William and Sprog cut a big, scary face in the side of the pumpkin shell.

Then they went down the garden to build the bonfire. There was lots of stuff to burn on it. Old raspberry canes. Dried-up potato and pumpkin plants. The prickly cases of the chestnuts, and dead leaves and dry branches from the tree.

By the time they had heaped it all up, the bonfire was taller than Sprog, and it was getting dark. Mam went back to the house, to get the food and the matches, and Sprog and William climbed up into the tree castle.

The bonfire looked exciting—but somehow not as exciting as it should have been. They stared down at it, not quite knowing what to say.

Then there was a funny noise from the house. Almost like a scream. Sprog looked nervously at William.

'Was that Mam?'

'Don't know.' William looked nervous too. 'Go up to the watchtower, Sir Stephen, and see if you can see anything.'

'Very lee, Sir William.'

Sprog scrambled up the rope ladder, settled himself and picked up the binoculars. Carefully, he scanned the windows of the house, but the curtains were pulled.

'I can't see anything.'

'Have another look,' said William.

Sprog scanned the house again, but there was nothing. He was just going to put the binoculars down, when he saw a light at the kitchen window. Two lights.

Red, then green.

'William! Mam's signalling. *COME AT ONCE. SOMETHING GOOD.*'

'Probably more mince pies,' said William. 'I'll go and help her carry them. You stay and keep watch.'

Sprog stared through the binoculars. It was too dark to see William walking up the garden, but he heard his feet, first on the grass, and then on the path.

A second later, the feet came back the other way. More of them this time. Mam must be coming too, with the food. Sprog reached for the torch that hung next to the binoculars and gave a quick flash of white light.

*WHO'S THERE?*

A red light shone back, from the bottom of the tree. *FRIEND.* Then Sprog heard someone climbing the rope ladder. Fingers tapped against the bottom telephone tin.

Sprog picked up the top tin and put it to his ear.

'Are you there, Sir Stephen?' said William's voice. It sounded a bit odd, but Sprog could hear the words all right. 'Come down straight away. Mam . . . Mam's going to light the bonfire.'

Very carefully, Sprog put the telephone tin, and the torch, and the binoculars back in their places. Then he climbed down the rope ladder.

William was sitting cross-legged in the middle of the platform. Sprog couldn't see his face, because it was too dark.

'What's Mam doing up here?' said Sprog. 'I thought she was going to light the bonfire.'

'I am,' Mam's voice said from down on the ground.

There was the scrape of a match, then a sudden, bright flare of light from the huge bonfire. And Sprog saw who it was sitting in the cabin.

'Dadda!'

He flung himself forward. Dadda grabbed him and hugged him hard.

'I did it, Sprog!' he said. 'They told me there wasn't a seat on the plane,

but I made them give me one. *If you
don't let me go back to my boys*, I said,
*I'll sit on the runway and stop the plane
taking off!'*

'And you got here!' yelled Sprog.
'You got here in time for Christmas!'

While the bonfire was cooking the
potatoes, they lit William's pumpkin
lantern and put it in the cabin. It
grinned mischievously at them as they
got everything else ready.

Mam sent up some rugs, to keep them warm, and then she loaded the food into the umbrella hoist. Baked potatoes, fresh from the fire. Scones and home-made raspberry jam. Pumpkin pie and hot mince pies. Sprog and William hauled them up and spread them all out on the platform.

'It's a feast!' said Dadda. 'A *midnight* feast!'

'I grew the pumpkin for the pie,' said William.

'That was where he hid my toffees,' said Sprog. 'When we were testing the telephone—'

'—and I told him to go up to the watchtower and look with the binoculars—'

'—like when I spotted the enemies we shot with green potatoes—'

'—and when I saw the signal about mince pies—'

'—that's what Mam fixed the rope ladder for—'

'—after Sprog picked the raspberries for the jam—'

'Stop! Stop!' Dadda put his hands over his ears and pulled a terrible face. 'It'll take me *weeks* to explore this castle. This must be the most complicated chestnut tree in the world. Telephones, watchtowers, hoists . . . And did you roast the chestnuts, as well?'

Mam grinned. 'We couldn't. The squirrels must have got them all. I didn't see anything except the prickly cases.'

'That's right,' said William.

Sprog didn't say anything. He just stood up and reached, very carefully, into the hole behind the cabin. His plastic bag was still there, and he pulled it out.

'Happy Christmas, Dadda,' he said. 'I saved these till you came.' And he tipped the chestnuts into Dadda's lap, in a shiny brown shower.

For a second, Dadda didn't say a word. He just gazed down at the chestnuts.

Then he looked up at Sprog and William, with dancing eyes, and growled a tremendous Ferocious Monster growl. 'Right! You're coming to roast chestnuts in the bonfire! The way I did with *my* dad. And if you don't like them, I'LL BOIL YOU IN TOMATO SOUP!'